Story and Art by
Sharean Morishita

"Thank you so much for picking up my book and reading it! This is my first colored printed comic so I'm super nervous...actually I'm always nervous....but that's okay because hopefully you all are able to have something fun to read despite me feeling so nervous about publishing this....I swear I'm a well adjusted adult.......Anywhoodle I hope you enjoy my silly little story!"

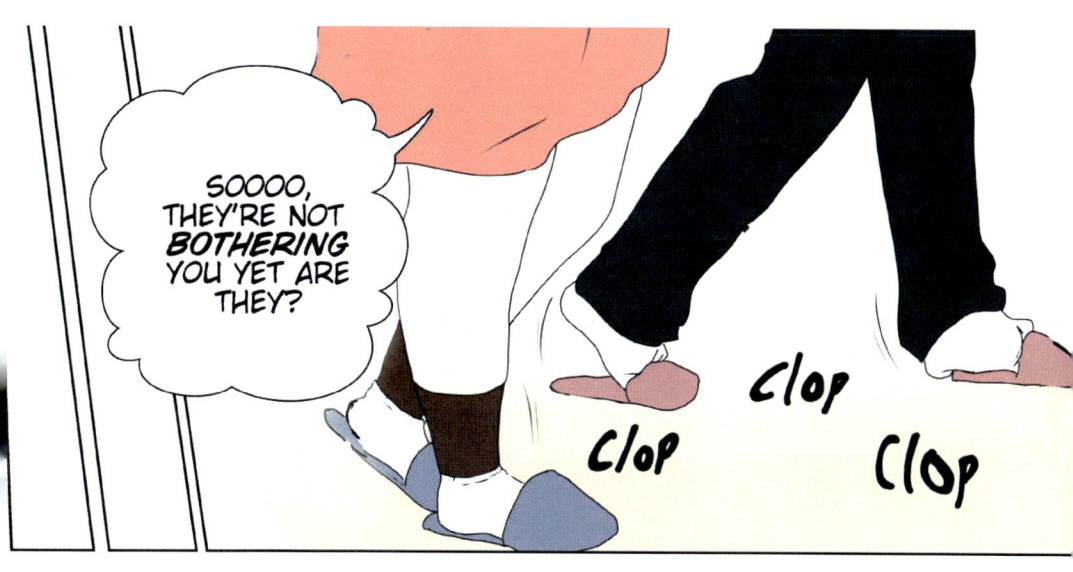

B-BUT DOESN'T IT FEEL UNCOMFORTABLE

SOCKS ARE SUPER RESTRICTING FOR THE MOVEMENTS OF YOUR TOES...

...

A-ACTUALLY...

YOU KNOW WHAT I THINK IS THE MOST ATTRACTIVE THING A HUSBAND CAN DO?

Gotta go big to bait him!

Episode 4

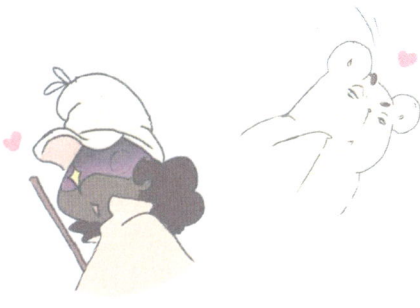

WORRY
WORRY
WHY IS HE BEING SO STUBBORN!?
DON'T CARE
NOD
NOD
I NEED TO BE THE STERN VOICE OF REASON....
JAE-HWA, LISTEN, IF YOU DON'T WANT TO TAKE THE MEDICINE....
COUGH
COUGH

THEN MAYBE YOU SHOULD GO HOME.

YOUR FAMILY WILL BE ABLE TO TAKE CARE OF YOU.

MY FAMILY WON'T BE BACK HOME TILL LATER THIS EVENING ...

IT FEELS COLD BEING ALONE IN AN EMPTY HOUSE.

I KNOW THIS IS ANNOYING AND SELFISH OF ME TO ASK BUT...

IF I TAKE THE MEDICINE... THEN...

DON'T CARE

...

THEN WOULD YOU BE OKAY WITH ME STAYING?

IT'S JUST WARMER HERE...

ORIANA, YOU HAVE TO COME FROM A POSITION OF STRENGTH

TELL HIM NO AND TO GO HOME ...

HE'S SICK

AND ALL ALONE...

OF COURSE YOU CAN STAY!

HER VOICE OF REASON HAS BEEN EASILY OVERPOWERED

Episode 5

* BRAIN'S OVER DRAMATIZATION
FLASHBACK
Can I Stay here with you, Plzzz~
SOB

BOOMPH

I SHOULDN'T HAVE SAID THAT.

SHE DIDN'T LAUGH AT ME RIGHT AWAY...

COUGH

BUT I KNOW IT'S COMING.

You don't like to be alone?

You're so clingy!

That's so lame!

You must feel so~o embarrassed!

I CAN FEEL IT.

IF I THINK ABOUT THIS LOGICALLY

THERE'S NOTHING WRONG WITH WHAT I SAID.

I JUST EXPRESSED MY FEELINGS...

IN THE MOST EMBARRASSING WAY POSSIBLE

SOB

SOB

COUGH

COUGH

DON'T CARE BEAR OUT OF ORDER

HERE SHE COMES.

PLOP

JUST STAY CALM.

Hmmmm

I SHOULDN'T TALK EITHER.

I WONDER IF I CAN I HELP DEFEND MY FACTION IN THE MIDDLE OF A RAID?

SHOOT!!

NO YOU HAVE TO WAIT TILL THE ATTACK ENDS.

THIS COLD IS MAKING ME WEAK...

BULLIES

MY GUARD LITERALLY JUST FELL... THOSE COWARDS.

IS SHE NOT GOING TO PICK ON ME?

JAE-HWA ...CAN I SEE YOUR FOREHEAD.

HERE IT IS! I KNEW IT WAS COMING!

WHY?

YOU'RE NOT SECRETLY UP TO SOMETHING?

WHY WOULD YOU THINK THAT?

"CAUSE OF THE SOCK INCIDENT."

"UH... THIS TIME IS DIFFERENT."

"..."

"I PINKY PROMISE!"

"THERE WE GO."

"THIS ICY PATCH SHOULD HELP."

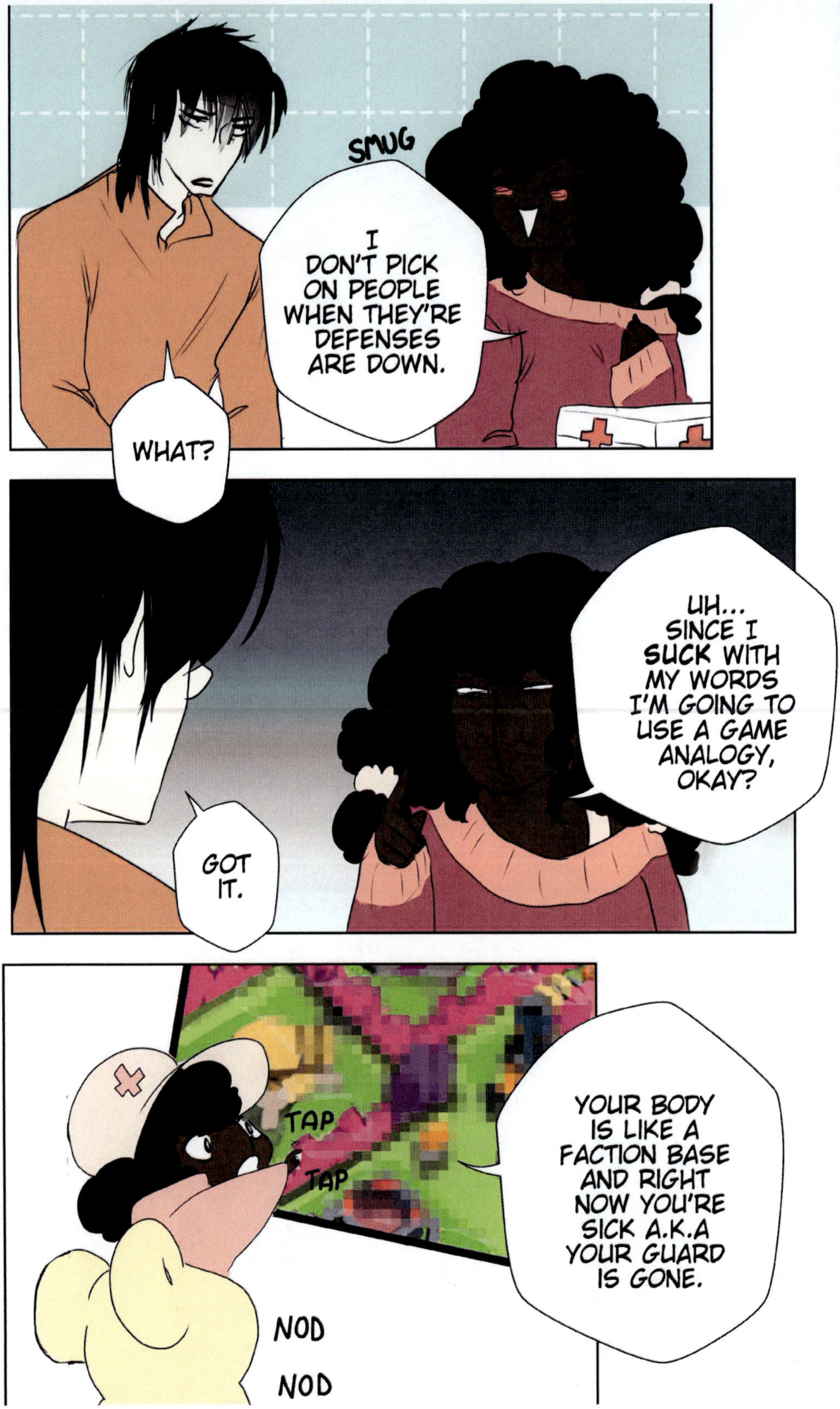
SMUG
I DON'T PICK ON PEOPLE WHEN THEY'RE DEFENSES ARE DOWN.
WHAT?
UH... SINCE I SUCK WITH MY WORDS I'M GOING TO USE A GAME ANALOGY, OKAY?
GOT IT.
TAP
TAP
YOUR BODY IS LIKE A FACTION BASE AND RIGHT NOW YOU'RE SICK A.K.A YOUR GUARD IS GONE.
NOD
NOD

AKA YOUR DEFENSIVE WALL HAS BEEN COMPROMISED.

IT'S NO FUN POKING A WALL THAT'S ALREADY FALLEN.

THAT ALSO INCLUDES TOYING WITH PEOPLE WHEN THEY'RE... VULNERABLE...

SO GET BETTER SOON SO I CAN START PICKING ON YOU AGAIN.

ARE YOU NATURALLY THIS NICE?

OR ARE YOU DOING THIS JUST BECAUSE OF THE SHOW?

HONESTLY IT'S A SPLIT 60-40.

...

Episode 6

HEY ORIANA ....
SO I'VE GOT A RANDOM QUESTION...
NOSEY
WHY ARE YOU STILL SINGLE?
OH GOD ...
...
HAVE YOU WATCHED THE SHOW I-
I DON'T WATCH YOUR STUFF, IT'S TOO LAME.
I....
OW

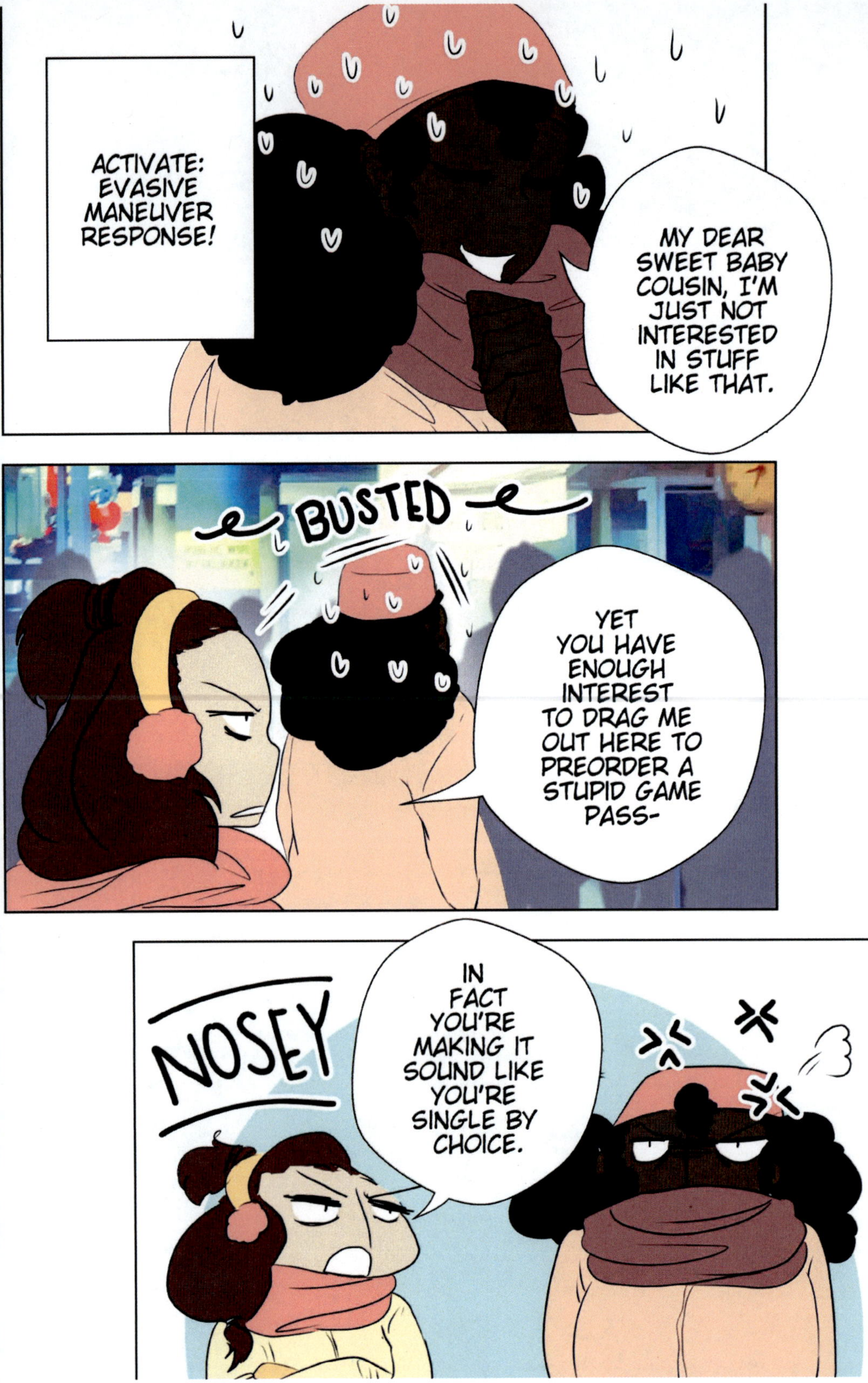
ACTIVATE: EVASIVE MANEUVER RESPONSE!
MY DEAR SWEET BABY COUSIN, I'M JUST NOT INTERESTED IN STUFF LIKE THAT.
BUSTED
YET YOU HAVE ENOUGH INTEREST TO DRAG ME OUT HERE TO PREORDER A STUPID GAME PASS-
NOSEY
IN FACT YOU'RE MAKING IT SOUND LIKE YOU'RE SINGLE BY CHOICE.

PETTY JOSEY

"YOU PROBABLY COULDN'T GET A GUY'S NUMBER EVEN IF YOU ASKED."

STAB

"LITTLE COUSINS ARE SUPPOSED TO BE SWEET; NOT BABY MONSTERS."

...

"PROVE ME WRONG THEN."

PETTY. PETTY PETTY ...

GO ASK THAT STUPID LOOKING GUY FOR HIS NUMBER.

!?

DAZED

FIRST OFF I DON'T HAVE TO PROVE ANYTHING TO YOU AND SECOND THAT GUY'S—

He isn't stupid looking...

I CAN'T DO THIS... I'LL HAVE AN UNFAIR ADVANTAGE SINCE HE ALREADY KNOWS ME.

IF YOU DO THEN I'LL BUY YOU THAT GAME PASS FOR YOUR STUPID GAME.

DEAL!

BUT FIRST I WANT SOMETHING TO GO ON THE RECORD...
I DON'T CONDONE THE MESSAGE THIS IS SENDING AND FURTHER MORE-
ZOOM
YOU HAVE SIXTY SECONDS
RING
RING
SIGH
HELLO?
IT'S BAD ENOUGH YOU PLAY THAT STUPID THING ON TV!

IT'S BAD ENOUGH YOU PLAY THAT STUPID THING ON TV!

...

I CAN'T HAVE YOUR FANS SEEING YOU BUYING THIS LAME CRAP ON YOUR FREETIME!

THAT PHONE CALL SOUNDED LIKE AN ANGRY SQUIRREL WAS YELLING AT YOU...

THAT WAS MY MANAGER

...

BUT HE'S MORE LIKE A SCREAMING BANSHEE.

"YOU'RE GONNA GET SICK DRESSING SO LIGHT LIKE THAT."

"..."

"GETTING THIS GAME PASS IS WORTH IT."

"ARE YOU HERE TO PRE-ORDER ONE TOO?"

"I'M CURRENTLY TRYING TO PROVE MY LITTLE COUSIN WRONG."

"..."

"SO I GUESS I'M NOT THE ONLY ONE YOU PICK ON?"

"MY GENTLE BULLY HAS NO RESPECT OF PERSON."

AND HERE I THOUGHT I WAS SPECIAL.
ACTUALLY YOU ARE BECAUSE YOU'RE THE ONLY ONE WHO CAN HELP ME WITH THIS BET.
BLUNT
YOU COULDN'T HAVE ASKED SOMEONE ELSE?
I WOULD HAVE BUT SHE WAS THE ONE THAT PICKED YOU.
WOW.... SO YOU DIDN'T EVEN PICK ME ON YOUR OWN.
THIS IS GOING TO SOUND MEAN BUT I'M KIND OF IN A TIME CRUNCH-

I GUESS IT'S TOO MUCH TO TALK TO ME-

YOU KNOW THAT'S NOT TRUE!

I'M GUESSING SHE DOESN'T KNOW THAT WE WORK TOGETHER?

...

...

I'M A COOL COUSIN RIGHT?

S-SHE SAYS IT'S TOO EMBARRASSING TO WATCH MY SHOW.

SO TO WIN HER STUPID BET I HAVE TO ASK FOR YOUR NUMBER.

THIS ISN'T JUST SOME ROUND ABOUT WAY OF *YOU* TRYING TO GET MY NUMBER?

DON'T WORRY I'M NOT INTERESTED IN THAT.

AGAIN OW...

SO HOW EXACTLY DID THIS BET START?

JAE-HWA... DO YOU UH- REMEMBER...

...

THAT *TINY* TIME CRUNCH I MENTIONED ABOUT EARLIER?

YOU WANT ME TO PLAY ALONG RIGHT?

I BASICALLY TOLD HER I'M SINGLE BY CHOICE AND SHE SAID I WAS LYING...

I'M KIND OF CURIOUS WHY YOU AREN'T INTERESTED IN RELATIONSHIPS...

AGAIN THE TIME CRUNCH...

IF THIS IS HOW YOU FINNESS A GUY YOU'RE DOING A WONDERFUL JOB...

CAN'T I TELL YOU LATER?

PANIC

I DON'T TRUST THAT YOU WILL.
BULLSEYE
IF I WIN I'LL SPLIT THE GAME PASS WITH YOU!
DEAL
DID YOU JUST NEED MY NUMBER OR BOTH MY NUMBER AND EMAIL?
JUST SAY SOME RANDOM NUMBERS AND I'LL WRITE IT DOWN ON PAPER.

WHY ARE YOU WRITING IT ON PAPER?

AH-HA! WRITING IT ON MY HAND WOULD BE WAY MORE BELIEVABLE!

YOU REALLY ARE TERRIBLE AT THIS.

. . .

**HANDS
PAPER**

. . . ? ? ?

GIVE ME YOUR PHONE.

Fine! Give me back my paper!

YOU STILL HAVE TO TELL ME THE REASON WHY AFTER THIS.

DON'T FORGET!

I WON'T!

AND HERE YOU GO LITTLE COUSIN~.

SO HOW DOES IT FEEL TO BE PROVEN WRONG?

WAIT.... WHAT ARE YOU DOING?

FWIP

CLUELESS

CALLING IT TO MAKE SURE IT'S HIS.

BLOCK

NO! DON'T DO THAT!

YOU DIDN'T JUST WRITE DOWN A RANDOM NUMBER AND MADE IT LOOK LIKE HE GAVE IT TO YOU DID YOU?

I KEEP FORGETTING HOW SMART SHE IS...

Ring
Ring

RING
SEE I KNEW YOU COULD NEVER-
RING
RING
RING
CLICK
HELLO?
IMPOSSIBLE!
HA!
PAY UP!
#TEAMWORK

Episode 8

Ring
Ring

CRACK

CRACK

WHERE'S ORIANA?

WHAT?

I DON'T SEE ORIANA.

CLANK

CLANK

CLASH

GUY'S CAREFUL WITH THE SUPPLIES PLEASE!

HER MANAGER CONTACTED ME ABOUT HER NOT BEING ABLE TO MAKE IT OR BEING LATE-

CRASH

GUYS CAREFUL WITH PUTTING UP THE GROCERIES!

SO... IS SHE NOT GOING TO BE HERE TODAY OR IS SHE JUST RUNNING LATE?

UH... I CAN'T REMEMBER BUT IT'S OKAY.

WE CAN JUST FILM YOUR HALF AND THEN—

AUGH!! GUYS C'MON, THE EGGS!!

...

YOU'LL BE OKAY FILMING BY YOURSELF RIGHT?

SURE...

PERFECT CAUSE TODAY YOU'LL BE MAKING COOKIES!

HE'S MAKING THEM BY HIMSELF?

YES, IT SOUNDS FUN RIGHT?

· · ·

NO.

CRACK

BWIP

IS SHE REALLY NOT COMING TODAY?

I SHOULD CALL HER TO FIND OUT...

→CLINGY WARNING ACTIVATED←

- Anxiety Alert -

WHAT IF SHE'S BUSY AND YOU'RE BOTHERING HER?

YOU'RE GONNA MAKE HER GHOST YOU.

why's he just standing there?

→ INITIATING DISASSOCIATION MANEUVER ←

YOU DON'T CARE.

POUR
POUR

CREW
CREW

MIX
MIX
MIX
MIX

That's enough mixing

SPLASH

CREW

YOU DON'T CARE

....

They're burning!

YOU DON'T CARE
....

CREW

YOU DON'T CARE...

It broke!

YOU DON'T-

SNAP
PLOP

Jae-hwa's ring tone

"One is the loniest number~"

"One is the loniest number~"

HE LOOKS SO MISERABLE

SIGH

ONE IS THE LONLIEST NUMBER
ONE IS THE LONLIEST NUMBER
CLICK
HELLO?
This is too sad to air!
Where's Oriana?
Why is that his ringtone!?
Oriana's Voice
GUESS WHO JUST GOT A 3 STAR WIN!
MY DRAGON ARMY TOTALLY JUST DEMOLISHED THIS PERSONS TOWN BASE!

...

DOOM

IS THAT WHY YOU'RE NOT HERE?

NO!

MY MANAGER DOUBLE BOOKED MY SCHEDULE.

She will feel my petty wrath

...

I WOULD HAVE TEXTED YOU

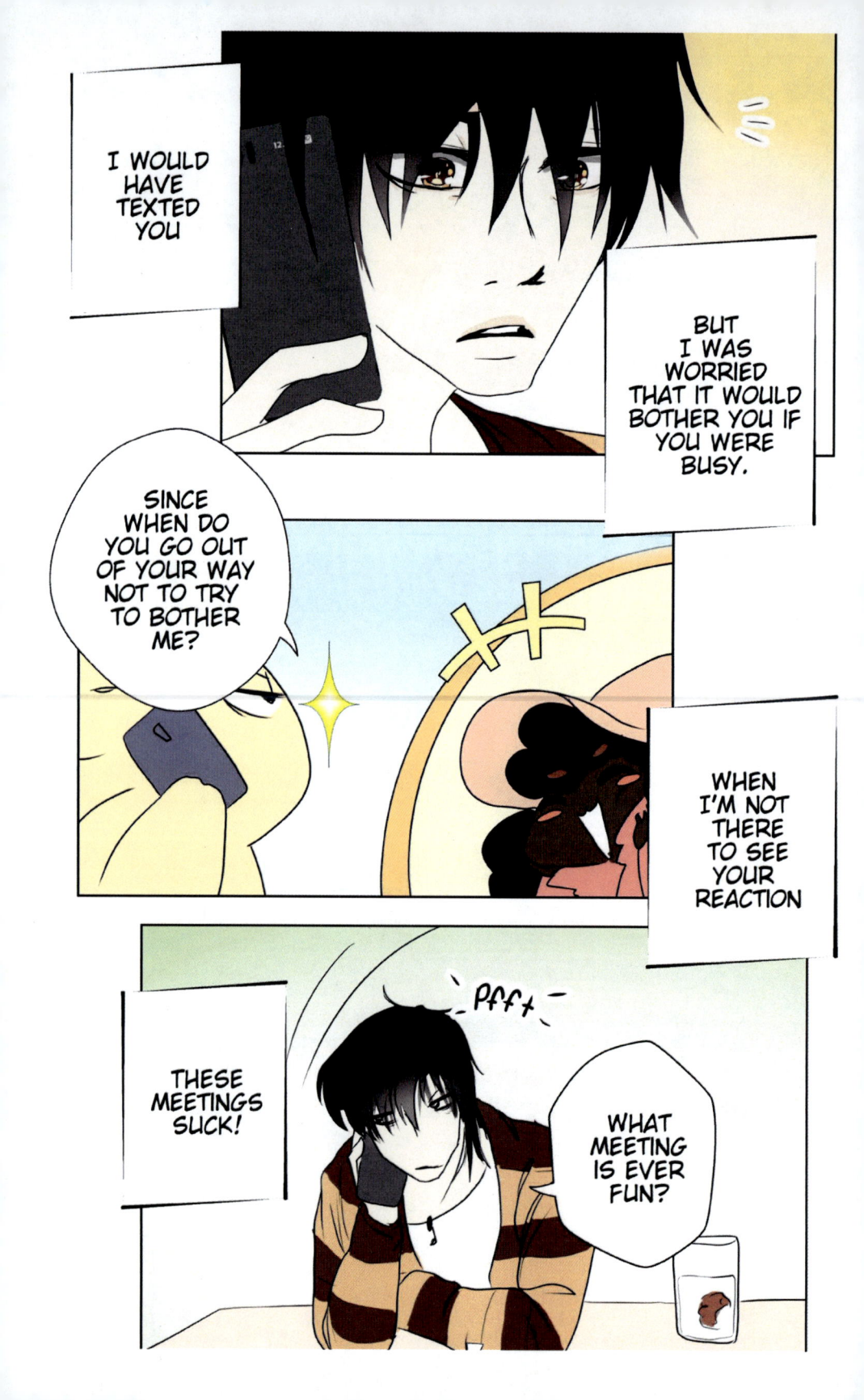

BUT I WAS WORRIED THAT IT WOULD BOTHER YOU IF YOU WERE BUSY.

SINCE WHEN DO YOU GO OUT OF YOUR WAY NOT TO TRY TO BOTHER ME?

WHEN I'M NOT THERE TO SEE YOUR REACTION

pfft

THESE MEETINGS SUCK!

WHAT MEETING IS EVER FUN?

ANYTHING FUN OVER ON YOUR SIDE?

...

NO...

IT SUCKS OVER HERE TOO.

THIS IS TECHNICALLY ALL YOUR FAULT.

UH-HOW?

HAD YOU FIRST LOOKED OVER YOUR SCHEDULE
THEN YOU COULD HAVE CAUGHT THIS
AND WOULD BE HERE RIGHT NOW.
-TSK-

WELL HIS WHOLE MOOD CHANGED

Episode 9

RAINY DAYS ARE SO BORING!

TODAY'S RATINGS ARE GONNA BE LOW IF WE DON'T DO SOMETHING...

OKAY BUT WHAT'S THERE TO DO THOUGH?

I ACTUALLY HAVE AN IDEA...

SUSPISOUS...

WHAT?

...

TELL ME WHY YOU'RE NOT INTERESTED IN RELATIONSHIPS.

TELL ME WHY YOU WANT TO KNOW?

I'M KIND OF CURIOUS WHY YOU AREN'T INTERESTED IN RELATIONSHIPS...
IF THIS IS HOW YOU FINNESS A GUY YOU'RE DOING A WONDERFUL
CAN'T I TELL YOU LATER?
BECAUSE YOU PROMISED YOU'D TELL ME.
AND WOULD YOU BE BOTHERED IF I DIDN'T TELL YOU?
I DON'T CARE...
TSK
BUT I WOULD FIND IT INTERESTING THAT YOU CAN MAKE AND BREAK A PROMISE SO EASILY.

LOOPHOLE

STALLING ISN'T TECHNICALLY BREAKING A PROMISE.

A FORMIDABLE OPPONET

IT TECHNICALLY ISN'T FULFILLING IT EITHER.

DOES IT BOTHER YOU THAT I'M STALLING?

AGAIN, I DON'T CARE.

....DO YOU REALLY NOT CARE OR IS THAT JUST SOMETHING YOU SAY?

SHOULDN'T YOU BE ANSWERING MY QUESTION FIRST?

HERE, PICK A RAINDROP.
WHY?
WHOEVER'S RAINDROP CROSSES THIS LINE FIRST GETS THEIR QUESTION ANSWERED FIRST!
HAVEN'T I ALREADY ANSWERED LIKE TWO OF YOUR QUESTIONS?

DOES THAT BOTHER YOU?
I PICK THIS ONE.

GREAT AND I'LL PICK....

THIS ONE!
FINISH LINE

I WIN!

ZOOP

↓ HIS

↓ HER'S

Shake Shake Shake

ORIANA... THAT'S NOT A FAIR WIN.

FAIR OR UNFAIR A WIN IS STILL A WIN!

LOOPHOLE!

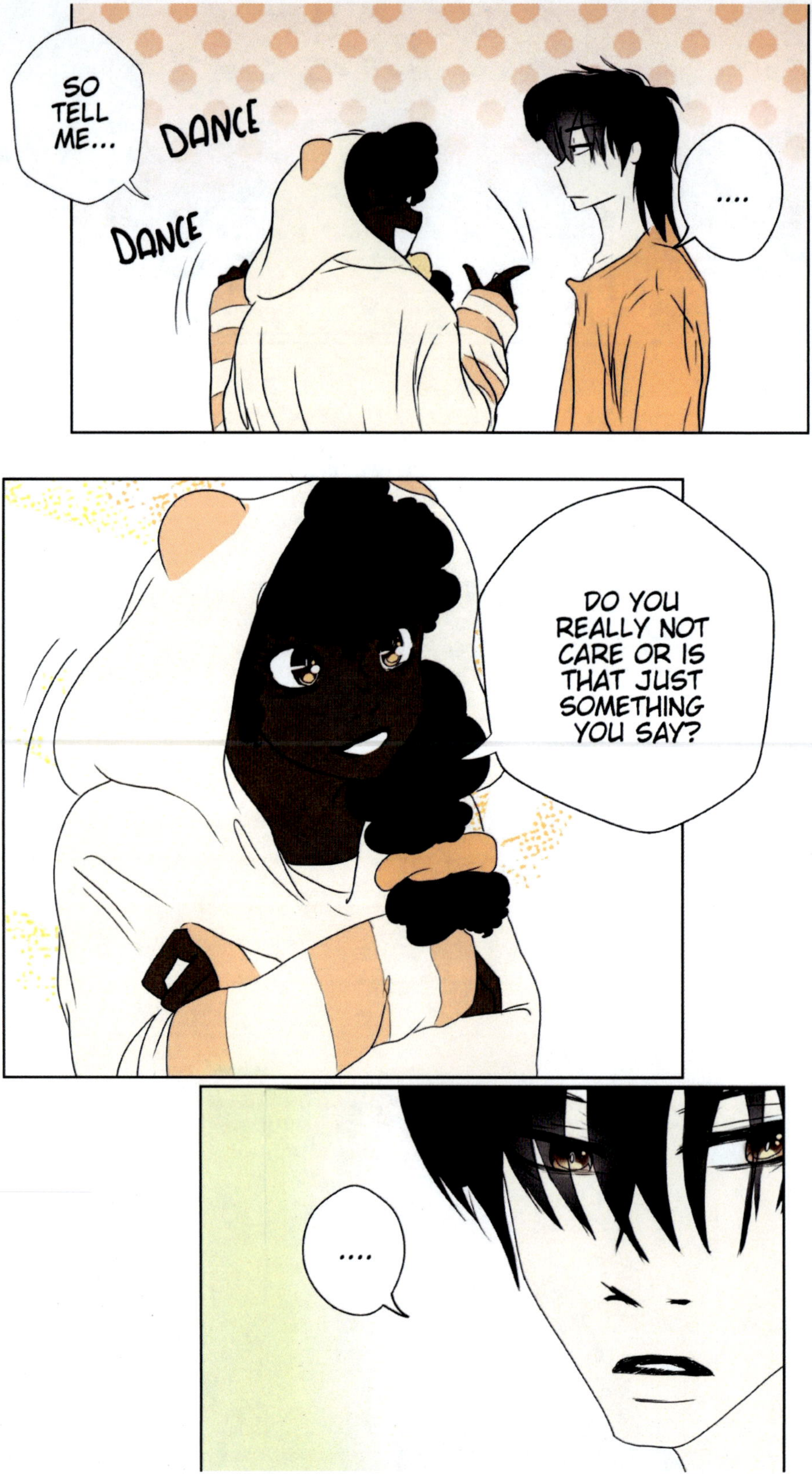
SO TELL ME...
DANCE
DANCE
....
DO YOU REALLY NOT CARE OR IS THAT JUST SOMETHING YOU SAY?
....

....

YES.

....

YES YOU DON'T CARE OR YES YOU'RE JUST SAYING THAT?

THAT SOUNDS LIKE ANOTHER QUESTION?

CAUSE THAT DIDN'T SOUND LIKE A CLEAR ANSWER.

"CLEAR OR UNCLEAR AN ANSWER IS STILL AN ANSWER."

FWIP

"...."

"JUST LIKE A WIN IS STILL A WIN."

"YOU'RE A BRAT."

"YES I AM."

Episode 10

・・・

HEY JAE-HWA...

TODAY'S YOUR DAY OFF RIGHT?

YEAH....

...

WHAT DO YOU WANT NOW?

I WANT YOU TO TELL ME WHY YOUR CO-STAR'S TEXTING YOU?

CAN YOU ...
LIKE NOT GO THROUGH MY PHONE?
AT LEAST ASK FIRST.
SNATCH
WHY IS SHE TEXTING YOU?
NAG
NAG
GIVE ME A SECOND TO READ IT.

YOU'RE NOT GOING TO TEXT HER BACK ARE YOU!?

UH-YEAH.
TSK

IGNORE
YOU SHOULDN'T TEXT HER ON YOUR DAY OFF!
WHY?
TAP
TAP
TAP

SCREAM
BECAUSE OF THE NO DATING CLAUSE IN THE CONTRACT YOU BOTH SIGNED!
AND HOW IS TEXTING BREAKING THE CONTRACT?
Please put your hands down
That's how careers fall!
BECAUSE TEXT MESSAGES ALWAYS LEAD TO SOMETHING MORE.

SHE'S NOT INTERESTED IN THAT.

HOW DO YOU KNOW?

DID YOU ASK HER?

YES!

...
WHAT DID SHE SAY?
?
EH?
THAT SHE'S NOT INTERESTED IN THAT STUFF.
WHY NOT?
I DON'T KNOW!
WELL DID YOU ASK HER WHY?

YES!

AND WHAT DID SHE SAY?

SHE ASKED ME WHY I WANTED TO KNOW.

...WHY DO YOU WANT TO KNOW?
I'M DONE TALKING TO YOU.
OH YOU CAN TEXT HER BUT CAN'T TALK TO ME?
YUP!

SHE'S FUN TO TALK TO.
YOU ON THE OTHER HAND....
DON'T FORGET THE NO DATING RULE!
I DON'T CARE!
? ? ?

YOU BETTER CARE!
...
...
YOU BETTER STOP MICROMANAGING MY LIFE FIRST.
NO ONE LIKES A SMART ALECK!
AND NO ONE LIKES A BUSYBODY EITHER.
...

"DO YOU ALWAYS NEED TO HAVE THE LAST WORD?"

"That'll be $12.80..."

IGNORE

NAG NAG

FUSS FUSS

"NO."

"SIR, YOUR TOTAL IS $12.80..."

Episode 11

SINCE YOUR SCHEDULE IS CLEAR YOU'RE GOING TO COME THE STATION FOR THE MEETING.

YOU KNOW I'M SUPPOSED TO BE DOING SOMETHING WITH MY AUNT AND UNCLE AFTER THIS.

I TOOK THE LIBERTY SINCE THEY ALWAYS END UP BAILING ON YOU.

THIS TIME IS DIFFERENT.
NO! WE GO THROUGH THIS EVERY TIME!
YOU END UP MAKING PLANS WITH THEM AND WHAT ALWAYS ENDS UP HAPPENING?

THEY BAIL BECAUSE THEY'RE BUSY SPENDING TIME WITH EACH OTHER!

I'M TIRED OF YOU ALWAYS COMING TO ME WHINNING AND ASKING FOR WORK BECAUSE YOU DON'T LIKE TO BE ALONE!

DO YOU KNOW HOW ANNOYING THAT IS?

....

JAE-HWA?

YOU OKAY?

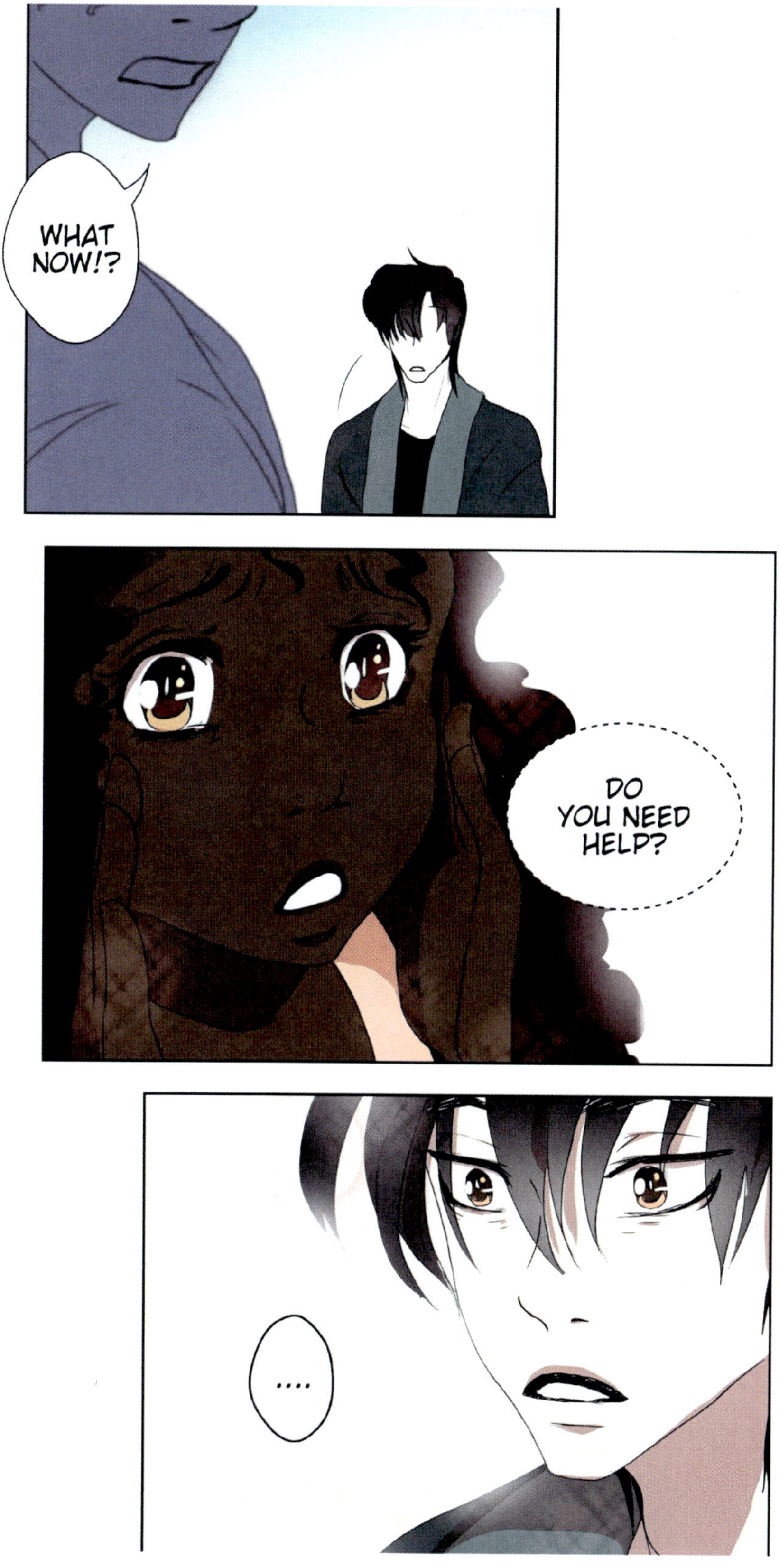
WHAT NOW!?
DO YOU NEED HELP?
....

JAE-HWA, DID YOU TELL HER TO COME HERE?
...
ACTUALLY MY COUSIN WORKS AT THIS CONVINCE STORE SO I STOPPED BY TO-
I'M WAITING FOR YOUR RESPONSE!
IGNORED
You gonna answer me?

ORIANA COME HERE.

IGNORED

EXCUSE ME?

WHISPER WHISPER

NOD NOD

HEY!

JAE-HWA HAS DECIDED TO PRIORITIZES HIS MENTAL HEALTH.

SO AT THIS TIME HE DOESN'T WANT TO COMMUNICATE WITH YOU ONE ON ONE.

PFFT

ARE YOU A CHILD?

WHISPER WHISPER

HE SAYS NO HE IS IN FACT 25 YEARS OLD.

"YOU'D KNOW THAT IF YOU'D VALUED HIM AS A CLIENT AND NOT JUST A TOOL TO USE FOR MONEY."

"HE DIDN'T SAY THAT!"

WHISPER WHISPER

"HE SAID HE GAVE ME THE LIBERTY TO SAY THAT."

FINE, YOU WANT TO BE PETTY...

TWO CAN PLAY AT THIS GAME!

SO YOU'RE THAT KOREABOO ORIANA, RIGHT?

A KOREA WHAT?

???

I'M HALF KOREAN SO... HOW?

THAT'S MRS. ORIANA.

PULL

? ? ? ?

WHAT KIND OF GUYS ARE YOU INTO?

What's your type?

PUSH

PULL PULL

NOT YOU.

STAY OUTTA THIS!

WHISPER WHISPER

NOD NOD

SHE SAID SHE'S FLATTERED BUT NOT INTERESTED.
THAT'S NOT WHAT I MEANT!
IMMA NEED YOU TO REGULATE YOUR TONE WHEN SPEAKING TO HER.
MAY I ASK WHY YOU AREN'T INTERESTED?

SHE WANT'S TO KNOW WHY DO YOU WANT TO KNOW?

WHISPER WHISPER

ANSWERING A SIMPLE QUESTION ISN'T GOING TO KILL HER.

GET ON YOUR KNEES AND SAY PRETTY PLEASE FIRST.

!?

PFFT

GETTING YOUR KNEES A LITTLE DUSTY FROM BEGGING ISN'T GOING TO KILL YOU EITHER.
Kee Kee Kee
YOU'RE BOTH CRAZY!!
I'M DONE!
TEAMWORK!

Episode 12

LATER THAT DAY

THIS IS NICE.

THIS IS A GREAT DAY OFF.

I GOT POPCORN!

MOOD INTERRUPTED

SCOOT OVER.

shameless

SWEETIE.... ME AND YOUR UNCLE LOVE YOU VERY MUCH.

BUT IT'S BEEN SO LONG SINCE WE BOTH HAD A DAY OFF.

YEAH THE *THREE* OF US HAVEN'T HAD A DAY OFF SINCE LIKE FOREVER.

YOU GUYS WENT OUT OF TOWN WITHOUT ME LAST TIME TOO.

TELL HIM

YES... BUT THE THING IS.

YOU ARE LITERALLY NOT DOING THIS TO ME AGAIN.

TELL HIM!!

SWEETIE TRY TO UNDERSTAND WE LOVE YOU BUT-

YOUR THIRD WHEELING IS KIND OF KILLING OUR COUPLE VIBE.

WE LOVE YOUR COMPANY WE JUST DON'T REALLY NEED IT.

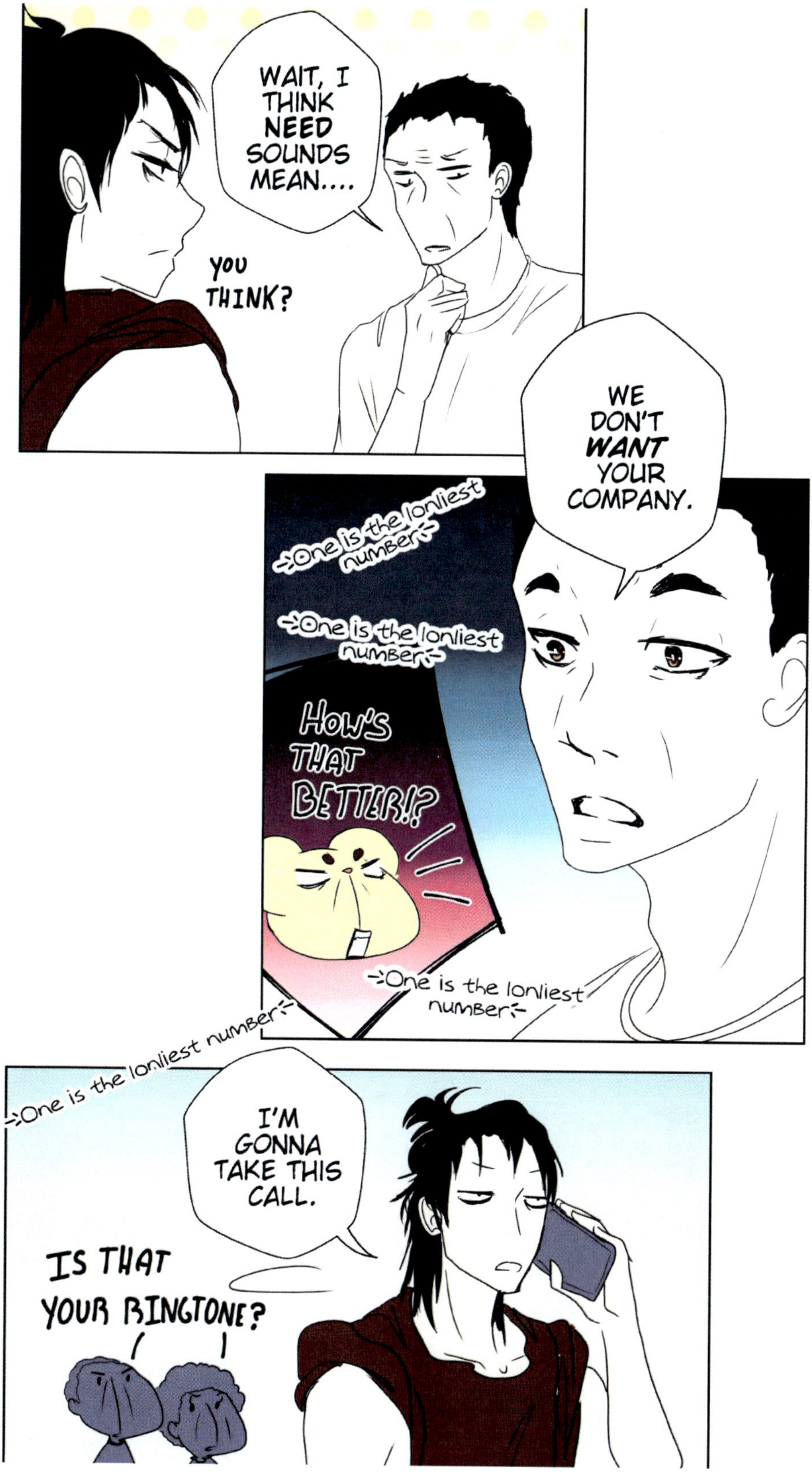
WAIT, I THINK NEED SOUNDS MEAN....
YOU THINK?
WE DON'T WANT YOUR COMPANY.
One is the lonliest number
One is the lonliest number
HOW'S THAT BETTER!?
One is the lonliest number
One is the lonliest number
I'M GONNA TAKE THIS CALL.
IS THAT YOUR RINGTONE?

BUT DON'T LET THAT STOP YOU TWO FROM FIGURING OUT MORE HURTFUL WORDS TO SAY.

HELLO?

NICE GOING!

WHAT!?

THIS STATION MEETING COULD HAVE BEEN SENT IN AN EMAIL.

OBIANA?

....YOU KNOW THAT MEETING WASN'T MANDATORY?

PFFT

REALLY!? MY MANAGER TOLD ME IT WAS!!

MAYBE WE WERE A LITTLE HARSH.

WE HARDLY GET TO SPEND TIME ALONE TOGETHER.

I KNOW BUT WE'RE ALL HE HAS.

HE'S SAD...

Pitiful...

Clingy...

THAT'S TRUE...HE DOESN'T HAVE A SINGLE FRIEND.
WITHOUT US HE'LL FACE A DANGEROUS COLD LIFE ALL ALONE.
?
?
...
?
I GOTTA GET OUT OF THIS MEETING SOME KIND OF WAY.
BLAH
BLAH
SOUNDS LIKE YOU GOT A PLAN COOKING.
YUP AND IT'S KIND OF LAME YOU'RE NOT HERE.

IS THIS YOUR WAY OF SAYING YOU NEED ME THERE?

-=PFFT=-
NO!

I DON'T **NEED** YOU HERE.

I **WANT** YOU HERE.

THERE'S A DIFFERENCE.

I FEEL SO SORRY FOR HIM SINCE HE'S SO *SAD* AND *LONELY.*

I *GUESS* WE CAN *AT LEAST* SPARE HIM A FEW HOURS.

AUNTIE, UNCLE I'M HEADING OUT!

WHAT?!

I GOT A MEETING AT THE STATION.

I thought that wasn't mandetory.

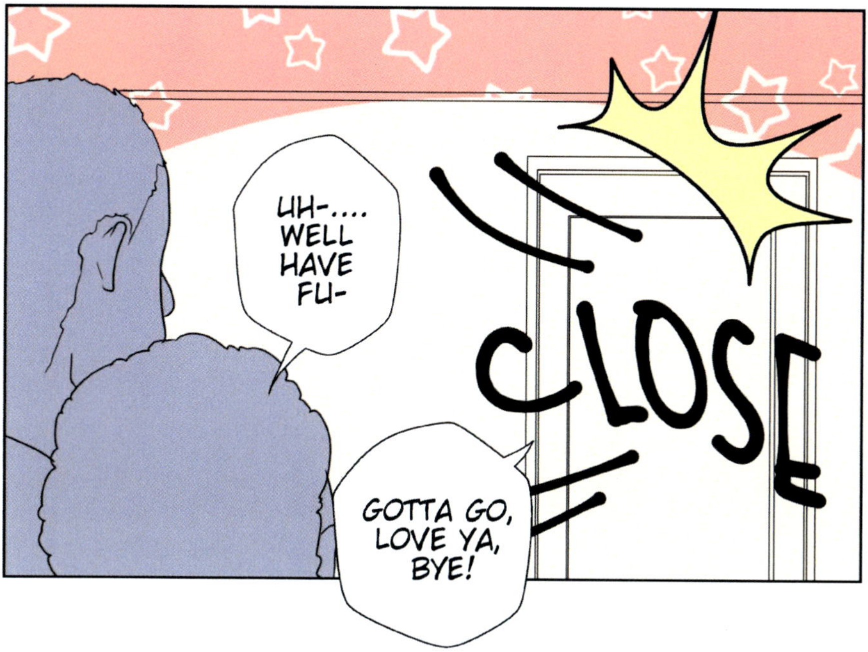
UH-....
WELL
HAVE
FU-
GOTTA GO,
LOVE YA,
BYE!
CLOSE

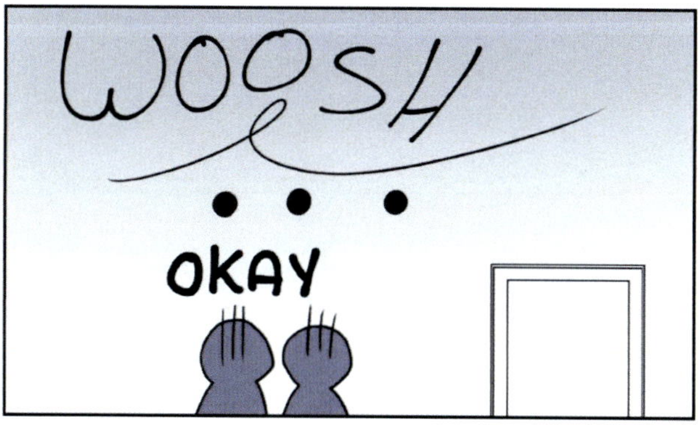
WOOSH
• • •
OKAY

Episode 13

LOOK WE GOT A PACKAGE!

WHO'S IT FROM?

IT SAYS "FROM YOUR SECRET ADMIRERS" ....

...YOU GOT ANOTHER FAKE HUSBAND I SHOULD KNOW ABOUT?

WHY DO YOU THINK IT'S ME!

TAP TAP

TELL YOUR SECRET **LOVERS** NOT TO SEND PACKAGES TO OUR FAKE **HOME**.

IT COULD BE FOR YOU!

WAIT, LOOK!

FLIP

THE BACK OF THE NOTE SAYS IT'S FROM OUR FAN GROUP!

They even printed out some of their online comments!

THOSE SNEAKY HOMEWRECKERS

WAIT? I'M EASY?

I'M SCARY ???

SO YOU DON'T HAVE ANY SECRET BOYFRIENDS?

IF I DO THEN ITS NEWS TO ME.

GOOD THAT MEANS I DON'T HAVE TO MAKE A SCENE.
?
??
SOMEONE SOUNDS BOTHERD
IS THAT A PASSIVE AGGRESSIVE WARNING I SENSE?
OH, PLEASE I DON'T MAKE THREATS.

I MAKE GUARANTEED PROMISES.
SO PETTY. (JUST LIKE ME♥
THEN I'D TOTALLY MAKE A SCENE FOR YOU TOO.
#CHAOTIC TWINS
I'M CURIOUS TO KNOW WHAT KIND YOU'D MAKE.
I'D BE SAD FIRST ...
AND I'D CRY...

THEN I'D SERVE YOU DIVORCE PAPERS WHILE PLEADING UP TO THE HEAVENS TO GIVE ME VENGENCE.

I'M JUST KIDDING!

I WOULDN'T DO SOMETHING SO OVERLY DRAMATIC

I'D HAVE MY MANAGER DO IT FOR ME.

Don't test me

AW LOOK THEY EVEN PACKED US COUPLES MASK.
SO WHAT IF A FAN ASKED YOU OUT?
I'M NOT INTERESTED IN STUFF LIKE THAT...
SO DOES THAT MEAN YOU'D SAY NO?

WAIT WHAT ABOUT YOU SAYING YOU DON'T CARE ALL THE TIME?
YOU KNOW THIS COULD EASILY BE SOLVED IF WE BOTH JUST ANSWERED WITH A SIMPLE YES OR NO.
NOD
HOW ABOUT WE BOTH ANSWER AT THE SAME TIME?
NOD
OKAY THEN ON THE COUNT OF 3.

OKAY SO THE QUESTIONS ARE WOULD YOU OR WOULDN'T YOU AND DO YOU OR DON'T YOU?

GOT IT!

1

2

3

YES!

...

WHICH YES WAS IT?

THEY'VE BOTH OUT WITTED AND DUMBFOUNDED EACH OTHER

Episode 14

THANK YOU SO MUCH FOR COMING TO THE FANSIGNING!
IT'S REALLY NICE TO FINALLY MEET EVERYONE!

I'M YOUR BIGGEST FAN!
REALLY? THANK YOU SO MUCH!

I REALLY APPRECIATE YOU SAYING THAT!

YOU'RE TOTALLY DIFFERENT THAN ON AIR!

CUSTOMER SERVICE MODE: ACTIVE

YOUR PERSONALITY ON THE SHOW...

REALLY SUCKS!

NO OFFENSE.

POW

BUT WE'RE SO GLAD THAT'S JUST AN ACT!
KYAAAA
AHH
AWWW-HOW SWEET...
YOU REALLY DIDN'T HAVE TO SAY THAT.
KEEP THE MASK ON!
NEXT IN LINE PLEASE!
KEEP THE LINE MOVING!
KYAAAA
GLOOM
CREW
CREW

CAN YOU SIGN THIS?

SURE! WHO SHOULD I MAKE IT OUT TO?

WRITE "TO MY FAVORITE ONE AND ONLY ETERNAL LOVE."

...

...

FWIP

ORIANA... WHAT ARE YOU PLOTTING?

WHAT? ♥

THIS IS THE PERFECT POKE THE BEAR OPPORTUNITY.

KYAA ♥ ♥ ♥

ORIANA! WE THOUGHT YOU COULDN'T MAKE IT TO THE FANSIGNING CAUSE OF A SCHEDULING CONFLICT!

...

I'M JUST POPPING IN REAL QUICK TO ANNOY MY DARLING~

KYAAAA ◇ SHAMELESS ♥ ♥ KYAA

THANKS DEAR...
YOU'RE WELCOME SUGARYPOP.

YOU SNUCK OUT TO GET THE NEW GAME PASS DIDN'T YOU?
ZIP YOUR LIP AND I'LL GET YOU ONE.
OK

SO...ARE YOU TWO SECRETLY DATING, LIKE FOR REAL?

OF COURSE NOT!
FWIP
WE'RE ALREADY MARRIED!
YOU PRECIOUS RUDE BEANS!
FWIP
SO OBVIOUS...
AREN'T YOU GUYS WATCHING OUR SHOW?
LOOM

I TOLD YOU THEY'D STAY IN CHARACTER FOR THE FANSIGNING!

GUYS THE LINE!!

DARN IT!

I WATCH IT!

AT LEAST WE WATCH IT.

FIRST MY COUSIN NOW OUR FANS

WAIT SO DO YOU THINK HE CARES ABOUT YOU OR IS IT JUST AN ACT?

HE BETTER OR ELSE I'M QUESTIONING THIS WHOLE MARRIAGE!

HE'S LOOKING AT US LIKE WE'RE HOMEWRECKERS

... SO DO YOU OR DON'T YOU CARE?
GUYS THE LINE!
DO YOU!?
DO YOU CARE!
DON'T BOTHER HE'S JUST GONNA SAY I DON'T CARE AGAIN.
OF COURSE.
OMG! HE SAID IT!

NOT SO FAST...

???

OF COURSE YOU DO CARE?

OR OF COURSE YOU DON'T CARE?

HE ALMOST TRICKED US!

SO CHILDISH...

HEY!

SECURITY! LINE CHECK PLEASE!

CHECK MATE.

Episode 15

WORK'S FINISHED!

BRING ON THE FAMILY COOKIE QUALITY TIME!

FAMILY UNIT! THE FIRST BORN IS HOME!

WHY DO YOU KEEP CURVING THAT NICE LOOKING YOUNG MAN ON YOUR SHOW?

GRAMPY....WHO TAUGHT YOU THAT WORD?

I DID.

GRRR...

OH.... SO YOU WATCHED MY SHOW?

SURE DID....

AND I SAW SOMETHING ELSE INTERESTING TOO...

....SO ABOUT FAMILY COOKIE NIGHT—

FWIP

HEY!?

DON'T TRY TO CHANGE THE SUBJECT YOU CON-ARTIST!

WHY AREN'T YOU INTERESTED IN RELATIONSHIPS?

BECAUSE PEOPLE SUCK AND SHOULD BE AVOIDED AT ALL COST!

OUR RAY OF DARKNESS IS HOME.

DUCKIE DID THE COOKIE ORDER COME IN?

YEAH I—

HOW DARE YOU AND THAT STUPID MASKED BOY SCAM ME OUT OF A GAME PASS!

What stupid masked boy?

COME AGAIN?

YOU'RE SEEING THAT WEIRDO YOU WORK WITH OFF THE CLOCK?!

WHAT ABOUT YOUR NO DATING CONTRACT!?

PLENTY OF PEOPLE LIKE YOU SO PICK ONE!

ARE YOU NOT INTERESTED BECAUSE YOU DON'T THINK ANYONE LIKES YOU?

AUNTIE DID THE COOKIE ORDER COME IN?

I THINK YOUR COUSIN KRISA HAS THEM.

I WANT SOME GRAND BABIES!
ZOO
YOU ALREADY HAVE ALL OF US!?
DUCKIE TECHNICALLY YOU DON'T COUNT....CAUSE YOU'RE NOT RELATED BY BLOOD.
!?
WHERE ARE YOU KRISA ??
NO... YOU GUYS ARE ALL BIG...
AND OLD NOW...
FWIP

STOP PICKING ON DUCKIE!

KIDS LISTEN TO GRAMPY!

PAY BACK MY GAME PASS!

GET HER!

HOW AM I SUPPOSED TO BE *GREAT* IF I DON'T HAVE ANY *GREAT*-GRANDBABIES?

VAIN OLD MAN...

KRISA! COOKIES!

GAME PASS

BABIES

ORIANA'S HOME.

NO DATING

...

SHUT-UP! HERE!

MUNCH MUNCH MUNCH

TAP TAP TAP

YOU ALREADY OPENED IT?

I JUST GOT AN EMAIL FROM CORPORATE ABOUT A 100 DAY SPECIAL.

THEY MIGHT DO A SECOND SEASON!

YOU ATE SO MANY...

RUDE!

HUG

I STILL CAN'T BELIEVE YOU GOT HER MIXED UP IN THIS VARIETY SHOW NONSENSE!

IT'S NOT NONSENSE, IT'S BUILDING A FAMILY BUSINESS!
WE'RE ENTREPENERS

THERE'S ONLY ONE LEFT.....
BICKER
YELL
NOISE
BICKER

I'M BUILDING OUR FAMILY LEGACY!
LISTEN TO GRAMPY
BUILD IT A DIFFERENT WAY!
AND SOMEONE ALREADY ATE HALF .....

I'M LEAVING.

WE STILL HAVE TO GO OVER NEXT WEEKS SCHEDULE!

DON'T CARE

YOU BETTER BE LEAVING TO BUY ME A GAME PASS!

YOU BETTER BE LEAVING TO MAKE ME A *GREAT-*GRANDPA!

YOU BETTER NOT BE!

DOES NO ONE CARE ABOUT FAMILY COOKIE NIGHT!

Episode 16

WOW DAD YOU REALLY WENT ALL OUT WITH DINNER!

YOU KNOW MY SAYING: "ONLY THE BEST FOR MY FAMILY."

CAN I HAVE-

YOU'RE GOING TO EAT WITH FRIENDS...

NO.

THIS IS FOR THE ROMANTIC DINNER I HAVE PLANNED FOR YOUR MOTHER AND I.

SO SELFISH ...

WHAT'S JAE-HWA GONNA EAT?

HE'll STARVE!

YOUR COUSIN HAS A MEETING AT WORK SO HE'LL EAT THERE.

IT FEELS LIKE YOU AND MOM ONLY CARE ABOUT EACH OTHER...
WHAT GAVE YOU THAT IMPRESSION?
HOW COULD YOU EVEN THINK THAT-
FWIP
HONEY! I'M HOME...
...
GET OUTTA HERE YOUR MOTHER'S HOME!

WHAT ARE YOU DOING HERE?

THANKS UNCLE

GUESS WHO'S MEETING GOT CANCELED!

ROMANTIC

THESE ARE FIRE HAZARD.

FWIP FWIP

ROMANCE

NO, THEY'RE ROMANTIC CANDLES.

HERE USE THIS INSTEAD.
IT'S MY SPONSORED DON'T CARE BEAR NIGHT LIGHT.
...
THATS NOT ROMANTIC.
YOU ALREADY COOKED DINNER?
TAKE A HINT ...
...
A ROMANTIC DINNER FOR TWO, YES....
THERE'S HARDLY ENOUGH FOR A FAMILY OF FOUR.

I'M ACTUALLY GOING OUT TO EAT WITH SOME FRIENDS...

DON'T LEAVE ME WITH THEM

WHY DON'T YOU TAKE YOUR COUSIN ALONG WITH YOU?

OPPS

NO- I MEAN WHY?

CAUSE I ONLY COOKED DINNER FOR TWO.

THEN MAKE MORE.

I RAN OUT OF FOOD!
GREAT IDEA DEAR!
WHY DON'T YOU TWO GO TO THE STORE TO GET MORE FOR US?
...
OR BETTER YET WHY DON'T YOU GUYS GO CAUSE I'M GOING OUT TO EAT WITH MY FRIENDS-
...
SINCE YOU'RE ALREADY GOING OUT TAKE YOUR COUSIN WITH YOU!
NO I WANT TO GO BY MYSELF!
HE'S A THIRD WHEEL!
JUST WATCH HIM FOR 1 HOUR!
NO!
THIRD WHEEL THAT NEEDS BABYSITTING

THIS IS JUST A HUNCH SO CORRECT ME IF I'M WRONG BUT...

I'M GETTING THE FEELING MY PRESENCE IS A BURDEN...

WE CATEGORICALLY DENY THAT!

FAMILY HUG

Your presence is wanted!

WHAT ABOUT ME BEING A BURDEN?

WE DENY THAT!

WAIT... A... SECOND...

YOU DIDN'T SAY YOU *CATEGORICALLY* DENY IT THOUGH!

OPPS

HE CAUGHT THAT ...

YEAH I DID

WAIT! IT'S NOTHING PERSONAL!

WE JUST WANT ALONE TIME WITH EACH OTHER!

OR OTHER PEOPLE IN GENERAL!

SAY LESS...

Episode 17

GRAMPY, I'M SATISFIED WITH MY LIFE THE WAY IT IS RIGHT NOW!
WELL I'M NOT SATISFIED WITH YOUR LIFE THE WAY IT IS RIGHT NOW!
WHY NOT?!
CAUSE YOU'RE PICKY, ALL ALONE *AND* SINGLE!

OKAY BUT I'M NOT SAD OR UNHAPPY SO...
WHY DO I NEED TO BE WITH SOMEONE?
CAUSE I WANT GREAT-GRANDBABIES.

WELL THAT'S NOT A GOOD ENOUGH REASON FOR ME.

TRY AGAIN

AHHH

DON'T YOU YOUNG PEOPLE ENJOY THE PHYSICAL RAMIFICATIONS OF LOVE—

THAT'S **NOT** MY LOVE LANGUAGE!

LET ME MAKE THAT CLEAR!

GRAMPY'S SORRY...

POPS GIVE IT A REST.
SHE'S NOT INTERESTED RELATIONSHIPS.
YAY YOU FOUND THEM!
SO WHAT!
I DON'T UNDERSTAND WHY YOU DON'T WANT TO BE IN A RELATIONSHIP!?
THAT'S LIKE ASKING SOMEONE WHO'S FULL AT THE DINNER TABLE WHY AREN'T THEY EATING MORE?
I SHOULD GET FOOD FOR DINNER...

IT'S NOT GONNA KILL YOU TO GET A SECOND HELPING!

GRAMPY, I DON'T WANT A SECOND HELPING!

BUT YOU HARDLY ATE!

I'M FULL!

FAMILY FIGHT?

NO!

EAT MORE!

KIDS NEVER EAT..

TABLE OF LIFE

COME AND DINE

THERE'S MORE LEFT ON THE DINNER TABLE OF LIFE THAT YOU'RE MISSING OUT ON!

NOT EVERYTHING ON THE DINNER TABLE NEEDS TO BE EATEN THOUGH!
THE AUDACITY
I'M OLD ENOUGH TO EAT WHAT I WANT, WHEN I WANT!
GRAMPY I'M A BIG GURL!
NO! YOU'RE A BABY!
WELL THAT'S TOO BAD BECAUSE WE EAT ALL OUR FOOD IN THIS HOUSE!
WELL THEN MAYBE I'LL JUST FIND MY OWN HOUSE!
HUH ...
!?
RING
RING
RING

PERFECT TIMING JAE-HWA! WHAT'CHA DOING?
FWIP
POPS!
SHE'S BLUFFING!

BUYING MORE DINNER SUPPLIES TO BRIBE MY FAMILY INTO SPENDING TIME WITH ME.
Do you need help?
SUP.

SINCE MY FAMILY IS TRIPPING I'M RUNNING AWAY FOR LIKE LIKE 15 MINUETS, WANNA JOIN ME?

MAKE IT AN EVEN 20 AND I'M IN.

BET

#

ORIANA WHY ARE YOU LEAVING WITH THAT DON'T CARE BEAR!?

ACK

...

BECAUSE I CAN EAT HOWEVER MANY SERVINGS I WANT AROUND HIM AND NOT GET HOUNDED ABOUT IT!
GIVE THE ANALOGY A REST.
LET ME BE FREE!

CAUSE HE'S DOESN'T CARE ABOUT ANYTHING!
THAT SOUNDS AWFUL!
Do you really NOT CARE or ARE YOU JUST SAYING THAT?
... YES SIR.

Episode 18

I'M GOING TO STAND OVER THERE AND VENT TO THAT INANIMATE OBJECT FOR A MOMENT.

OR... YOU COULD VENT TO A LIVING BEING THAT CAN LISTEN?

IT'S NOT ALWAYS GOOD FOR OUR MENTAL HEALTH WHEN PEOPLE DROP THEIR UNSOLICITED DRIBBLE IN OUR LAP.

I VOLUNTARILY GIVE YOU MY CONSENT TO DROP YOUR DRIBBLE ON ME.

DON'T SAY IT LIKE THAT!

ALL I WANTED TO DO TODAY WAS TO HAVE A NICE FAMILY COOKIE NIGHT!

INSTEAD I ENDED UP GETTING INTERROGATED ABOUT BEING SINGLE....

I CAN'T BELIEVE MY GRAMPY CALLED ME PICKY!

I'm chaotic not picky!

DON'T SAY IT LIKE THAT...

I ACTUALLY HAVE A TYPE AND IT'S CALLED THE AWESOME PERSON TYPE.

THE WHAT?

IT'S A PERSON THAT'S EMPATHETIC AND NICE.

I KEEP A LIST.

VERY ORGANIZED

THAT SOUNDS LIKE YOUR TYPICAL BASIC HUMAN BEING...

The bar is so low

I have simple needs.

WELL APPARENTLY TO MY GRAMPY IT'S NOT.

HE THINKS THE REASON I'M NOT INTERESTED IN RELATIONSHIPS IS BECAUSE I'M OVERLY PICKY...
BUT THAT'S NOT TRUE ....

I'M ALREADY HAPPY SO WHY DO I NEED TO GET INTO A RELATIONSHIP?

I KNOW WHY I'D GET IN ONE.

REALLY? WHY?

KIND OF SHOCKED YOU'D WANT ONE!

DON'T SOUND SO SHOCKED

WELL MY REASON WOULD BE...

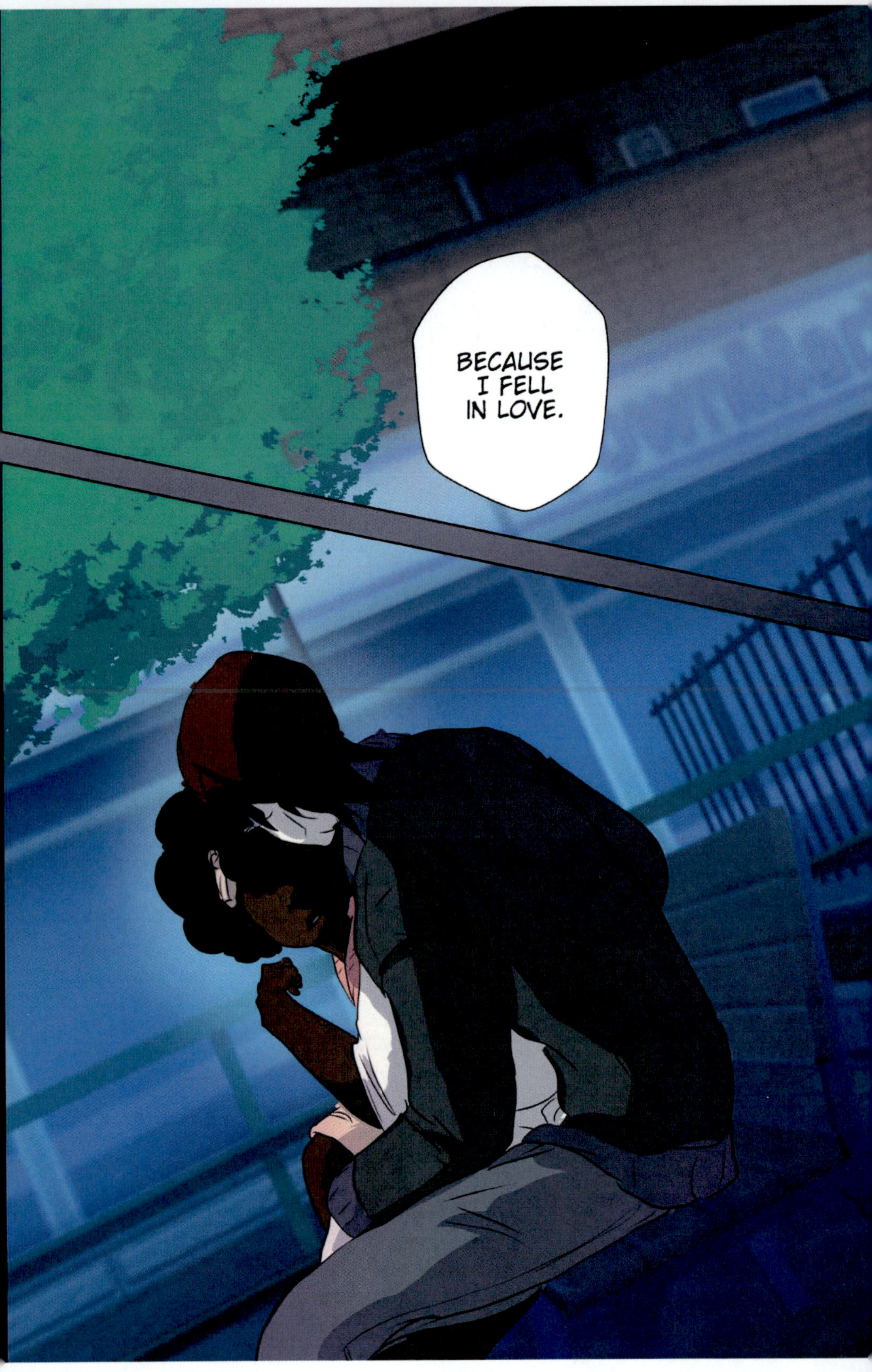
BECAUSE I FELL IN LOVE.

WELL I'VE NEVER EXPERIENCED LOVE LIKE THAT SO....

I FIND THAT HARD TO BELIEVE...

THERE'S A FIRST TIME FOR EVERYTHING.

WOW... DéJà VU ...

TRUE

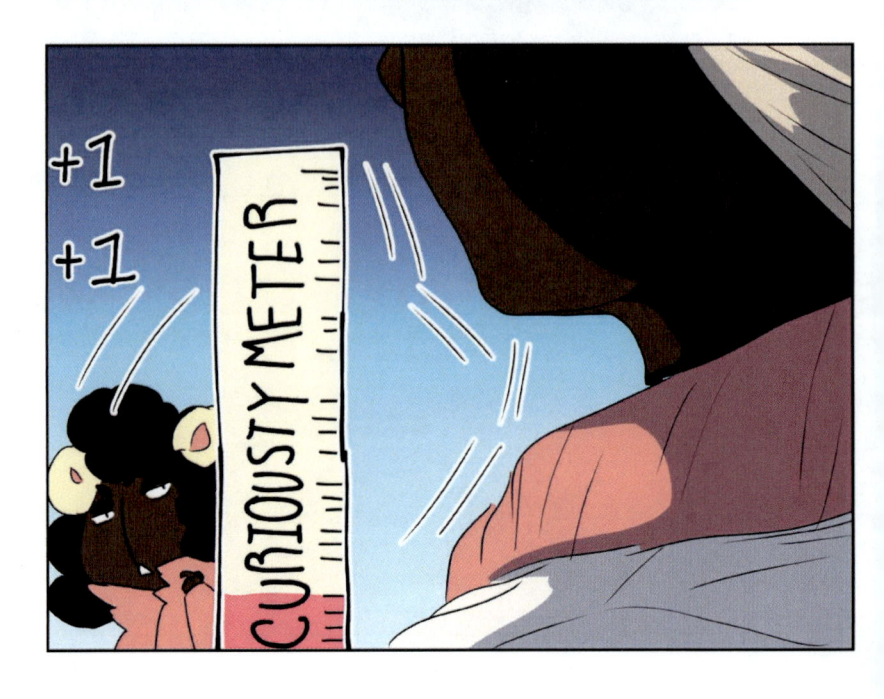

HOW WOULD YOU FEEL IF I SAID I THINK I COULD BREAK THAT?

+1
+1

CURIOUSTY METER

I WOULDN'T FEEL ANYTHING CAUSE YOU'LL BREAK WAY BEFORE I DO.

NEW CHALLENGE ACCEPTED.

-LET THE GAMES CONTINUE-

Catch Me! Fight Me! Love Me!

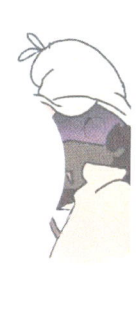

SEASON 1 END

Would you like to have a Volume 2?

DROP A COMMENT ON MY FACEBOOK PAGE OR WEBSITE TO LET ME KNOW!

I can never really tell if there are others that enjoy the stories that I create or if I'm just giggling at my own story jokes all to myself....

So if you'd like to see me do a volume 2 feel free to leave me a comment at S-Morishitastudio.com or find me on Facebook at S-Morishita Studio

---

Find me on my Social Media:
Twitter: @Sharean_M
Instagram: @smorishita_studio
Facebook: @Smorishitastudio
Website: www.s-morishitastudio.com

Special thanks goes to all of my patreon supporters both past and present! Thank you so much for sticking with me and my whacky stories for so long! I love you all so very much!
www.patreon.com/smorishita

For inquiries, email me at:
contact@s-morishitastudio.com

Made in the USA
Coppell, TX
29 September 2022